Come and See

To Ledlie and Roxana Laughlin—M.M.

To A. Yeager with affection—S.S.

Come and See · Text copyright © 1999 by Monica Mayper · Illustrations copyright © 1999 by Stacey Schuett
Printed in the U.S.A. All rights reserved. http://www.harperchildrens.com

Library of Congress Cataloging-in-Publication Data
Mayper, Monica
  Come and see : a Christmas story / by Monica Mayper ; illustrated by Stacey Schuett.
     p.   cm.
  Summary: Shepherds, townsfolk, and travelers celebrate the birth of Christ with a midnight feast and dance.
  ISBN 0-06-023526-8 — ISBN 0-06-023527-6 (lib. bdg.)
  1. Jesus Christ—Nativity—Juvenile fiction.   [1. Jesus Christ—Nativity—Fiction.]   I. Schuett, Stacey, ill.   II. Title.
PZ7.M47373Co   1999   93-45730
[E]—DC20   CIP
                                                                                                                   AC

Typography by Al Cetta · 1 2 3 4 5 6 7 8 9 10 · ❖ · First Edition

Come and See

A Christmas Story

BY MONICA MAYPER

ILLUSTRATED BY STACEY SCHUETT

HARPERCOLLINS*PUBLISHERS*

In the hills was sudden music
  Come see
  Come and see
The sheep and shepherds heard.

In winter night, a morning light
Come down the rocky road and see
In the cold, a new-bloomed rose.

In our sleeping town, the shepherds knock

Come see

Come out and see

Doors open slow, then wide.

Mother, Father, come and see!
Come where? See what?

Come see the world made new.
The same old world, but new.

We run to the innkeeper's stable
Come see
Come here and see
The shepherds lead the way.

It roofs a tender family
A new baby in the hay.

The mother's resting on the straw
Against the donkey's side
  Come see
  Come in and see
The oxen stamp their hooves and breathe
To keep the baby warm.

We children lift our lamps to see—
The townsfolk crowd behind.

See there, in the manger!
Look how the cattle guard him.

We watch the newborn baby
Swaddled in the hay.

The shepherds lay down skins of milk
The innkeeper brings out bread and wine.

It's time for joy and feasting!
But shhhh, he's fast asleep, now.
Come out and let them sleep, now.

In the chill air we eat and drink our fill
Glad at this midnight chance

Then

Slowly in the starlight
Come dance
Come now and dance

Shepherds, strangers
Travelers, townsfolk . . .

Quietly in the starlight
Come dance
Take hands and dance
We all begin to dance.

Around the sleeping baby
We all, together, dance.